Published in the United States

Edition 1

Summary. Penny Porter is a pitcher who learns lessons that not only apply to softball but also to life. An exciting, endearing story about a fastpitch softball pitcher with a big problem, a big secret, good friends, a new team, a mystery player, and a big game ahead!

Keywords: softball, softball fiction, softball story, fastpitch, fastpitch fiction, fastpitch story, Penny Porter, Sue Stone, Pitcher from Pine Hills.

Please visit us at www.softballstories.com
and stay up to date on
Penny Porter - the Pitcher from Pine Hills Series
and on other exciting books!

Artwork by Emmanuel Creations

ISBN 979-8-65430-471-1

This book is dedicated to:

All Fastpitch Softball Athletes,

especially

Elizabeth

Victoria

Katherine

Chapter 1:

Penny Porter is a seventh grader at Pine Hills Middle School, on Long Island in Pine Hills, NY. Pine Hills is a suburban community located near the center of Long Island. It has lots of parks, shopping, and kids who play sports. It also has kids with problems. Some of them have big problems.

Are you kidding me?

Penny thinks to herself as she is about to leave the bathroom stall.

Why me? What did I do to deserve this?

Penny wonders as she reads her name carved into the grey metal stall partition wall.

Why would someone take the time to carve my name and call me a pickle? It doesn't make any sense. I'm nice to everyone. Except maybe that nasty boy, Evan in Mr. Smith's class. He deserved what he got, but he couldn't even get into the girl's bathroom. So, it couldn't have been him.

Penny rubs her forehead with her hand and tries to come up with a way to remove the embarrassing artwork.

Everything was going great and now this! How am I going to get rid of this? It's carved right into the metal.

She tries the pen that is in her pocket. It doesn't work – it doesn't even make a mark.

This isn't fair. Who would do this? I'm going to need a sharpie to cover this up. That should work. I hope.

Penny Porter pushes the bathroom door open and hurries into the school hallway. She is wearing a tie-died pink and orange t-shirt that has big blue script lettering that says "SOFTBALL" with an outline picture of a girl pitching a softball using a windmill motion below it. In big red letters below that, it says "iPitch." Penny goes to Pine Hills Middle School, a school just like thousands of others. There is nothing special about this school: cement walls, lots of windows, and black and white tiles on the floors. There are of course lots of kids, ranging from well-behaved to out of control. There are lots of teachers too. Most are pretty good at what they do, but a few could use some refresher classes on how to teach middle school kids.

Penny hurries back to her class while thinking,

> *Mr. Jenkins gets aggravated when kids are out in the bathroom for too long.*

She hurries even faster and feels her face begin to turn red.

> *I hope he doesn't pick on me when I get back inside. I hate when he does that. I don't think I was gone too long – or was I?*

Slightly out of breath, Penny stumbles through the door making a bit of a racket. This gets Mr. Jenkins' attention. Mr. Jenkins is Penny's science teacher - a teacher who tries to make jokes about everythlng. He wears the same tan pants and dark red sweater vest over a plaid shirt almost every day. He's a real "fashionista."

"So glad you could rejoin us Penny! Maybe you can answer a question about the dinosaurs we are studying. What do you call a dinosaur that has stinky feet?"

Penny starts turning an even brighter shade of red as she navigates the classroom to find her seat.

"Umm. I don't know Mr. Jenkins. Look......I'm sorry I."

Mr. Jenkins cuts her off,

"It's called ex-stinked. Get it? Extinct. Dinosaurs are extinct so they no longer smell. Ex-stinked. Yes, well...."

Pretty much the entire class groans with yet another stupid Mr. Jenkins joke. Just as Penny takes her seat the bell rings to end the class. Penny sighs in relief that her school day is almost over. Thankfully, science is her last class.

Penny rushes out of the classroom, down the hall, past the gym, down the stairs, and over to her locker. She dials in her combination but doesn't get it right.

> *Always when I'm in a hurry! I hope no one saw my name in the bathroom. Oh no! Maybe it's been there for a while. Did everyone see it?*

She tries the combination again and this time opens her locker. She shoves her books in without a thought and grabs the black Sharpie on the top shelf. She slams the door closed and retraces her steps back upstairs to the bathroom. Everyone else is trying to get out of the building so they can go home or go to sports or some other fun activity. Not Penny. She is on a mission.

Clutching the Sharpie marker in her right hand, she plows through the old wooden bathroom door eager to get rid of the horrifying artwork someone obviously created to be mean to her. She is immediately greeted by an unpleasant smell.

Holy moly, what's that smell? I hope whatever made that smell is long gone and that stall is available. I don't want to have to wait for someone or I'll miss my bus,

she thinks to herself. As she gets closer, she sees that the stall door is open.

Oh, thank you!

But just as she is stepping to the door, she sees that an older girl she doesn't know is coming out. This older girl, wearing cut up jeans, a plaid shirt tied around her waist and a rock concert shirt on top that says "Ramones" on it, puts her hand out to shove Penny back. Penny notices a small gold ring in the girl's nostril.

"Watch it kid. What's your rush? You gotta go that badly?"

Penny puts the brakes on and almost crashes into the grey metal partition wall.

"Uhhh…. Sorry. I didn't see…"

The tall girl hunches over so her face is right up to Penny's face. The girl's black, pin straight hair falls forward and almost covers her eyes. Penny can smell the tuna fish the girl had for lunch, with a piece of it still stuck in her braces. The girl is so close, Penny can also see the blackheads on her nose, where she missed her lip with the bright red lipstick she is wearing, and the clumps of mascara on her eyelashes.

"Well open your stupid eyes and look where you're going, dumbo."

The girl flicks Penny's ear and stands up to her full height.

"Do you see me now?"

Penny backs up and gets out of the girl's way. Once the girl leaves, Penny runs into the stall and locks the door. She uncaps the Sharpie and starts scribbling over her name. It covers enough so that it's hard to tell what it originally said. For at least the tenth time today, Penny sighs with relief. This time, because she completed her mission. A teenager's life is hard!

your last year of 12u. Next year you move up to 14u. I really think you will do well this year. I can't wait to see how the other teams do against your new drop ball."

"Mom? Do I really have to? Maybe we can just look at a travel team instead? I heard there are some really good ones around here."

"Penny, travel teams cost lots of money. They also travel – something your dad and I can't do right now."

"The other coaches are so lame. They don't really coach at all. They just sort of treat their teams like Brownie troops. It's not softball at all - it's Scoutball. They have nice get-togethers and do lots of crafts and stuff."

"Well, I have a surprise for you Penny, but you'll need to register for Junior League to find out what it is."

"What, Mom? What is the surprise?"

"Can't say. You'll have to register first."

Mrs. Porter puts her hand to her mouth and twists it like she's locking a door with a key. Then she motions like she's throwing the key away. She picks up her papers and make sure she has the registration forms and Penny's birth certificate to prove she can play 12u softball.

Chapter 2:

Margo and Penny Porter arrive at Pines Hills Middle School and enter through the side door closest to the parking lot. Signs are posted on the doors that Junior League registration is being held in the cafeteria. They make their way through the hallways until they reach the cafeteria. Different registration stations are set up for both baseball and softball as well as different age groups. They find the station labeled "10u/12u Softball" and get on the line. There are well over 100 people in the room registering and the cafeteria sounds as noisy as it does when the kids are eating lunch – maybe noisier.

"Margo!"

A tall blonde woman shouts as she approaches the line. The woman is holding her daughter's hand and pulling her forward toward the line.

"Hi, Dianne. How are you. Wow, is this Elaine?"

Dianne nods her head,

"That's her."

"She must've grown six inches since last year."

"Well maybe four inches, but yes – she is sprouting up. Hi, Penny! You've grown too. Are you ready to play softball this year?"

Penny looks up,

"Hi Mrs. Amber, I've..."

Mrs. Porter cuts Penny off,

"She's been practicing the past few weeks with me in the backyard."

"Oh, that's right. I forgot – you used to play softball, didn't you?"

"Yes, I played in the very first Junior League World Series. As well as the next one too. We went all the way to win the Eastern Championship but lost due to a bad call in the World Series."

The line moves up.

"Well Margo, what team do you think Penny will be on this year. I'm hoping that Elaine is on Dr. Leery's team. He's so nice. His team feels more like a craft club than a softball team! The girls are always so close on his team."

Penny looks up at her mom with an "I told you so" look.

"Next!"

The league man behind the table shouted to try and get Mrs. Porter's attention.

"Hey Coach, you're up!"

Mrs. Porter broke away from her conversation with Mrs. Amber and addressed the league man.

"Hi Tim. How are you?"

"Great Margo. Looks like we're going to have a busy year this year! Lots of kids signing up and it looks like we'll have at least six teams for 12u – maybe more!"

Penny pulled on her mother's sleeve.

"Mom?"

"What, Penny?"

"Mom, why did he call you Coach?"

"See what you've done now, Tim?"

Smiling, Mrs. Porter faces Penny and says,

"Yes, this is the surprise I was talking about. Your Dad and I will be coaching the team this year."

Penny starts smiling and pumps her hand high in the air,

"YES! That's awesome!"

Mrs. Porter completes the registration, takes the paperwork and registration materials, and says goodbye to Tim, the league man.

"Mom, that's fantastic! Who is on our team?"

"Well Penny, there's a few kids from last year, but you mostly know the kids on our team."

"Is Gracie coming back to play?"

"No, I'm afraid she seems to have given up softball for good."

"What about Elaine Amber? Her mom will be heartbroken if Elaine isn't on Dr. Leery's Brownie team!"

"Uh, no – she's not on our team. In fact, I believe she is on Dr. Leery's team. She'll be very happy then."

"OK, so who?"

"Well, we have your catcher, Taylor Meyers."

"Awesome! She is a great catcher. We really is the best catcher around."

"Erica Muller is on our team."

"I know we need a few pitchers, but honestly, I don't think that girl likes me very much."

"She seems nice enough."

"Who else, Mom?"

"Alyssa."

"Rogers? Please say yes."

"Yes, Rogers. She's a pretty scrappy shortstop."

"That's awesome! I can't wait to play with Alyssa again."

"KK"

"Oh cool — Kayla Kim is an awesome outfielder. She can reach home plate all the way from right field."

"Jenny, your besty."

"No way! Jenny too. This is going to be the best year ever!"

"Julia Philips as another pitcher but also to play third base."

"OK. I don't know her all that well, but that's fine. What about M&M's?"

"Yes, Mary Mooney is on the team too."

"She's always bringing M&M's to practice, so that's cool."

"Debbie Branford as another catcher."

"Oh yeah, I remember her from last year. She's pretty nice. Although she seems to always get hurt."

"Hopefully, we can change that through some better coaching. We also have Andrea Wilson. I think you remember her from when you used to take dance class."

"Was she the girl with dirty blonde hair in pigtails?"

"Yes, but I don't think she wears her hair that way any longer. She's about a head taller than you too."

"We always got along OK."

"And the last player on our team is a new girl, Sue Stone. I don't know anything about her. She just moved here a few weeks ago."

"I hope she's good. Mom, when we get home can we look at my softball gear? I think I may need some new equipment."

"Sure. It's still in the garage."

The Porters make it home in a few minutes and enter through the garage.

"Here it is Mom. I found my softball bag. We already know I need a new glove. It's been hard practicing with you with such a tiny old glove."

"I think your bat may be too short and you can probably handle a heavier bat now too. I also want you to get a heart guard and a face mask."

"I knew you were going to insist on a face mask. I'm not a big fan of them. My hair gets caught every time I take it on or off."

"Get used to it, Penny. Next year the girls are so much bigger at 14u and you can really get hurt if a ball comes back at you."

"OK, I'll give it a try. I don't want to lose my teeth!"

Mrs. Porter closes the garage door and they both head inside. Mrs. Porter turns to Penny,

"I hope you liked the surprise, Penny."

"I do Mom. Thanks for doing this. I can't wait for the first practice!"

"It will be pretty soon. Why don't you wash up and I'll start getting dinner ready? Your Dad should be home with the twins soon."

"OK, Mom."

Penny skips along to the stairs and jumps up two steps at a time. She is floating and so excited to start her journey with her new team. She gets to the top of the stairs and takes a quick stop by the bathroom to wash her hands. She doesn't even think about what she's doing. Her mind is occupied with thoughts of her new team.

Then it hit her. The bathroom incident. It all came rushing back to her – her name carved into the bathroom wall: "Penny the Pickle."

> *I've got to FaceTime the crew and see if they know anything about this. This is horrific! I can't believe I have to deal with this now.*

Penny goes past her bed and sits at her desk. She opens her laptop computer. Once it boots up, she goes into FaceTime and starts a video chat with Alyssa and Taylor.

> "Hi guys. I've got some great news to tell you!"

Taylor, who seems very interested, says,

> "What's up Pen?"

"My mom and dad are going to be coaching a softball team this year, and you guys are on it!"

Alyssa, who is now all of a sudden very interested, speaks up.

"Wow, that's fantastic. No more Coach Demon! I really didn't like going to his practices. The games weren't bad, but the practices were ridiculous."

Taylor, equally interested, asks,

"Who else is on our team?"

"Us three, Jenny, KK, M&M, Julia, Erica, and a few others I either forgot or don't know very well.

Alyssa was shrieking the entire time Penny said a name.

"I'm not thrilled about Erica."

Alyssa shouted,

"She's a bit of a drama queen, don't you think?"

Taylor considers Erica and adds:

> "She's not a bad pitcher, and we need another pitcher due to league rules. Penny can't pitch every game you know."

Penny, in a more serious tone takes over the chat.

> "Guys, I need to tell you something and get your opinion about it."

Taylor giggles, and says,

> "Don't tell me we have that kid Jordan on our team! She is seriously out there. I don't think she even really knows how to play softball. All she seems to care about is hanging out at the mall. I'm not sure – but she might be on drugs."

> "No Taylor, Jordan is not on our team. This isn't about softball. This is something else. Something that happened to me at school today."

Alyssa, who is usually less serious than Taylor, asks Penny,

"Why? What happened today?"

"Well, I left boring science class today. We were going over dinosaurs. It seems like the same material we went over two years ago in fifth grade anyway. I went to the bathroom. You know, the older bathroom by the science classes on the second floor?"

Alyssa answers,

"Yeah Pen, we know that bathroom. What happened? Did some dork boy get pushed into the bathroom again like last week?"

"No, that's not it. I used the middle stall and just as I was finishing up, I noticed that my name and a cute rhyme were scratched into the paint on the wall."

"What did it say, Penny?"

Alyssa asks, almost afraid to hear the answer. As good friends, she knows that an attack on one of them is an attack on all three of them.

Penny replies, feeling embarrassed.

"It said Penny Pickle and had a picture of a pickle as well."

This time Taylor, feeling the importance of the situation, asks:

"What did you do about it? Did you report it?"

"No, I didn't report it. I tried to cover it with pen, but I couldn't even make a scratch in the paint. So... I went back to my locker after class and got a Sharpie. Then I covered the embarrassing artwork with black Sharpie. You can't tell what it says anymore."

Taylor jumps in very concerned,

"That's not good Penny. Who could've done that? Why would someone do that? Everyone seems to like you!"

Penny responds,

"That's why I FaceTimed you guys – to see if you have any ideas of who could have done this or why?"

Taylor tries to think of who could be responsible,

"I don't know Penny. Maybe it was that awful girl Tara. She hasn't liked you since fourth grade. Then there was the kid with the scissors. What was her name? Daniella or something."

Taylor tries to remember the kid's name - the kid with the scissors. The kid who cut other students' hair off during recess. Yes, Daniella Prianti was her name. She got suspended for a long time for that stunt.

"No, I don't think it was either of them. I haven't talked to Tara in more than a year. I'm not even sure if Daniella still goes to Pine Hills. Maybe they moved or something. I know she wasn't very happy with me for telling Mr. Durbin what she did...."

Penny can hear her sisters making a racket as they obviously just got home and her dad talking loudly to her mom. Mrs. Porter calls from downstairs,

"Penny!"

Penny ends the conversation,

"Sorry guys, my mom is calling me to dinner. I've got to go. Please think about who could have done this to me. I really need to know what I'm dealing with here. I'll see you both at school tomorrow."

"Don't worry, Penny. We're here to support you. We'll figure this out, one way or another."

Chapter 3:

The entire Porter family hops in Mr. Porter's car, a big black Ford Explorer sport utility vehicle that always smells like popcorn from all of the popcorn kernels that have fallen between the seats. They drive over to their favorite sporting goods store, Sports Source. This is a small, but busy store on the main street in Southport.

Penny is anxious to go shopping for new softball gear and is the first through the door. Her footsteps cause the old wooden floorboards to creak as she walks in. She immediately recognizes the old familiar smell of the store. It smells like old wood, dust, and old leather – maybe a little spilled coffee too. The rest of the Porter family catches up and makes it into the store. Mr. Porter has a different experience upon entering - a pleasant smell of plastic and vinyl greets him, as does the store owner.

"Hello Porter family! How is everyone doing today?"

28

Mr. Porter responds,

"Great, John. Thanks. How are you and the family?"

John, a retired fireman, comes around the counter and shakes Mr. Porter's hand:

"Everyone here is fine, thanks. What can I do to help you folks today?"

Mrs. Porter responds,

"Matt and I are running a team this year and Penny needs some equipment for the new season. She seems to have outgrown almost everything in her bag."

John, who is surprised by the news says,

"Wow, you guys are going to run a team? That's great news. It's just what our town league needs — some new people to shake things up a bit."

Mr. Porter chimes in laughing,

"That's us! We're great at shaking things up. We're so good at it that things may never be the same again."

Mrs. Porter playfully taps her husband on the arm,

"C'mon Matt. This is going to be great!"

Mr. Porter has his doubts if coaching a team is a good idea,

"I know. That's what you keep telling me."

Mr. and Mrs. Porter look at each other and John can tell that there have been some important discussions around the topic of coaching. He finally breaks the awkward silence,

"Penny, can I help recommend any equipment for you?"

Penny turns toward John and becomes excited all over again at the thought of shopping for new equipment!

"Yes, please. I need a new bat and a new glove!"

Mrs. Porter quickly adds,

"And a facemask and a heart guard for protection. Right, Penny?"

"Right, Mom."

John starts walking toward the glove section.

"Right this way, Penny. I have a great glove in mind for you. I think you're going to really like it. I just got a few of them in."

John grabs a beautiful white glove off the rack and hands it to Penny.

"This is the Rawlings Liberty Advanced glove. It was modeled after the famous Oklahoma pitcher, Keilani Ricketts. It's just like the glove she used to win the Women's College World Series!"

Penny grabs the glove and puts it on. It's a bit large.

"What size is this glove?"

John, looks at the size printed on the glove,

"It's a twelve point five inch glove. It may be a little bit big, but if you take care of this glove, it will last you through high school and maybe even college. Let's have a look at it."

John looks at the glove and sees that the adjustments on the glove don't get small enough to secure the glove on Penny's left hand. He grabs a batting glove off of the rack and hands the left batting glove to Penny.

"Here put this on underneath the glove. Let's see if that helps."

Penny slips off the big white Rawlings glove and puts on the tight batter's glove. Once the batter's glove is on, she puts the white Rawlings glove back on. This time it fits correctly and can't easily fall off.

"That's perfect now. Wow – this glove is long. I won't miss catching any balls with this glove! It's beautiful."

Mrs. Porter comes over and checks the fit of the glove and then takes the glove off of Penny's hand and tries it on herself.

"Wow, this is a nice glove!"

John points over to the bat section and Penny follows him over.

"Let's see what size bat you need, Penny."

John gives Penny a few different bats to try. He measures how heavy a bat Penny can hold out parallel to the floor at shoulder height. Then he has her swing a few different bats and observes her bat speed and form. He gives Penny a fairly heavy bat and she has a hard time swinging it. The bat drops as she swings, and her bat speed slows way down.

"Ok Penny, I think we've got the right size and weight..."

John looks over toward Penny's parents and announces,

"You need a 32" long bat with a minus 11 drop."

Penny looks confused.

"What's a drop?"

John smiles and explains,

> "Well, it's a measurement of the length of the bat in inches minus the weight of the bat in ounces. So, a 32" long bat with a minus 11 drop, will weigh 21 ounces. If you bought a minus 10 drop bat, the bat would weigh one more ounce, so it would weigh 22 ounces."

Penny nods her head that she understands. John picks up a nice colorful bat and inspects the end knob for the size and weight.

> "Here Penny, try this bat. This is a really great bat. It's the new DeMarini composite bat in your size and weight."

Penny takes the bat, looks around to make sure she won't hit anyone, and swings the bat a few times. She smiles and then examines the barrel of the bat. She runs her hand over its surface and looks at all the bright colors. She reads the writing on the bat and spins it over in her hands. John walks over to a different area of the store and returns with a heart guard and a metal facemask.

"Here's a facemask and heart guard in your size."

John puts the items together on the counter, while Penny is still looking at the bat. Mrs. Porter comes over.

"Wow, that's a nice bat. We never had anything that cool to play with when I was a kid. John, that bat looks really expensive."

John moves behind the counter and replies,

"Well, it's the best there is. Yes, it's expensive, but Penny is going to hit some homeruns with this bat. Aren't you Penny?"

Penny smiles at her mother.

"Of course, I am. It's perfect. I can't wait to hit some balls with this!"

Mrs. Porter shrugs her shoulders and decides not to argue about the cost. She is just happy that Penny is excited to play.

The door opens and Jenny Carson and her father walk in. Penny puts the DeMarini down on the counter next to the pile of other softball gear she is getting. She runs over to see her friend and teammate, Jenny. She gives her a quick hug and the two walk away from their parents a bit so they can talk. Penny notices that Jenny is wearing her softball jersey from last year. It is a green jersey with the word "Tigers" printed in yellow script on the front. It has her last name "CARSON" printed in capital letters on the back as well as her uniform number – 27 in giant yellow numbers. Penny starts the conversation,

"Hi Jenny, what are you doing here?"

"I need to get a new glove. What about you?"

"Me too, but I need a new everything."

Penny laughs and point over to the counter.

"I'm also getting a new bat. My mom insists that I wear a heart guard and a facemask too. Not my choice, but I guess I need to start getting used to them."

Jenny scrunches her eyes up as she did not consider a facemask or heart guard.

"Hmm. I guess I'm gonna need those too. I've seen a lot of the 16u and 18u girls wearing them. They look kind of stupid, but I don't want to get hit in the face with the ball. That would probably really hurt!"

Penny turns serious and pulls Jenny closer as they walk further away from their parents. Mr. and Mrs. Porter are now laughing with Mr. Carson about something. When they get a reasonable distance away, Penny turns her back to the adults and speaks in a very low voice – almost a whisper.

"Jenny, I have a problem I want to tell you about, but you have to promise me you won't tell anyone, OK?"

"Sure Penny. Of course. You know you can trust me. What's wrong?"

Penny licks her lips and thinks of the words to describe her problem. She describes finding the "artwork" on the bathroom wall and how she scribbled it out using a Sharpie.

> "Jenny, did you see it? It was on the second floor in the bathroom by the science classrooms."

Jenny takes a few seconds to think about the last time she used that bathroom.

> "No, I don't remember seeing it. I used that bathroom not too long ago. No one I talk to mentioned seeing it either. You know we have a lot of blabbermouths in our school, so you can pretty much bet that if someone saw it, they would say something about it. They probably wouldn't be too nice about it either."

Penny is relieved, and sighs quietly.

> "Well that's good. Maybe no one actually saw it. I spoke with Taylor and Alyssa last night and we tried to figure out who could

have done it. We didn't really come up with anyone."

The door to the store bursts open and sounds like it's breaking with a loud crash and a girl practically falls through the doorway. She struggles to keep herself from falling flat on her face. She lands on one knee and looks around to see if anyone saw her less than graceful entry.

Penny and Jenny turn around as they are startled by the loud noises coming from the front of the store. They look at each other and then back to the girl who is now trying to regain her balance and stand upright.

The girl dusts her knee off and straightens the dark shirt she is wearing. She smooths down her dark wavy hair. The girl seems to be about the same age as Penny and Jenny, but she seems somehow bigger. Not taller. Not fatter. Just bigger. Penny considers the girl.

> *This girl seems really strong and muscular. I bet most of the boys at school would be afraid of her! But wow – what a klutz!*

The girl is followed in by her father. He is also wearing all black: a black t-shirt with some rock band on it, black pants, and black boots. He completed the look with a long, pointy beard – maybe 6 inches long or so.

They stop and talk to John for a second, who points toward the bat section. The two move off to the other part of the store. Penny can hear part of their conversation.

The girl's father, concerned about his daughter asks,

> "Susan, are you OK? That was some entrance you made there."

The girl doesn't answer. She just weakly smiles at her father and keeps walking. Her father's question confirms her own concerns that she looked clumsy and stupid coming in the store's front door. She noticed the two girls staring at her and wished they weren't there to see her flop around like a seal.

Penny and Jenny turn their attention back toward each other. Jenny looks up at the ceiling and tries to think who has a grudge with Penny or doesn't like her. She could only think of one person.

"The only one I can think of is Erica. She's had a beef with you since last year when you were named top pitcher in the league and starter on our last team. I never heard her say anything bad about you, but then again, I don't talk to her that much. She's not that funny or interesting to hang around with. In fact, I think she's kind of irritating. I have seen her kind of roll her eyes every time you get picked to pitch. Then she stares at the ground and looks like she's moping."

Penny looks confused and doesn't understand why someone would write bad things about her on the bathroom wall.

"Do you think she really hates me that much?"

"Look Penny – you're the number one pitcher. She's a pitcher but she's number two. Number two isn't number one. You pitch more than she does. The coaches always call on you, not her."

Penny considers this and reasons with her friend,

"OK, but she also pitches. She also gets playing time. We can't run a team with just one pitcher. The rules don't allow me to pitch every inning of every game. I'm not sure I could do it, even if it were allowed. I get that I pitch more than she does, but it isn't that much more. Is the difference enough for her to hate me?"

"Like I said before – you're number one. You have the reputation of being the best. You're an amazing pitcher and she's just a good pitcher. Yes, we need another pitcher, but she doesn't get the fame you do. I don't really know her well enough to judge whether she would do this or not."

Mr. and Mrs. Porter pay for the new equipment and start moving toward the door to leave. They look around for Penny. Mr. Porter yells over to Penny.

"Come on Pens lets go. It's getting late."

Penny looks back at Jenny with a worried look.

"Thanks for helping, Jenny. I'll let you know if I figure anything out. Please don't tell anyone."

"Of course, Penny. I'll pay attention to see if anyone Is talking about this too."

Chapter 4:

Penny looks up at the big clock on the wall and sees the class is almost over. English is Penny's least favorite class as she finds it tedious and boring. She watches the second hand on the clock ever so slowly spin around the dial.

> *Only a few more minutes until this class is over! I can't take it anymore. Today's lesson is more boring than usual. I hope I don't fall asleep or start drooling. Just a few more seconds to go. I think I can do it. Just a few...more...seconds...to go. OMG, this is taking FOREVER. I wish I liked English more so this wouldn't be such torture. Almost there, then I get to go to lunch! I love lunch! I'm so hungry! I hope they have something good today, like lasagna! I forgot to look at the lunch menu last night. Whatever it is, I'm going to get one of those packs of chocolate chip cookies too.*

I can't wait for practice today. Our FIRST practice! Yay! I get to see all my friends and see how the other kids on the team mesh in too. I hope everyone gets along and the new girls aren't lame. That wouldn't be good. If they are OK, then we will have a really fantastic team! Thankfully, Mom and Dad will be our coaches. This is going to be great. No more Coach Demon!

The bell rings! Penny snaps out of her daydreaming and packs up her notebook. She races out of the classroom and begins navigating toward her locker. The halls are packed with kids seemingly going in every direction. Kids are screaming, yelling to each other, and one is even singing. Penny aims herself toward the righthand wall and gets bumped over and over as kids are heading in the other direction, off to their next classes.

Finally, she gets to her locker, but there are so many kids coming by she has a hard time dialing in her combination. For a second Penny isn't sure if she remembers the combination! Her cheeks turn red and she takes a deep breath.

Oh yeah, it's 34 right, 3 left, and 15 right. I can't believe I almost forgot that! I gotta wake up!

Penny tosses her books into her locker, slams the door shut, spins the combination knob a few times, and sprints off toward the cafeteria. The crowd thins out as she approaches the cafeteria. Just as soon as she gets inside the cafeteria doors, she gets on the lunch line.

A tall, geeky boy in tan pants and a white shirt is behind her. He's looking at a comic book, snorting and laughing to himself. There's a shorter girl in front of her that she has seen before - but doesn't know her name. Penny who is staring straight ahead, lets her gaze drift downwards and notices the unnamed girl has a really bad case of dandruff. There are white flakes all over her shoulders and back. She doesn't smell too good either. Penny scrunches her face up with revulsion.

OMG, this girl stinks! Doesn't she know she smells bad? She must know. Someone must've told her. What is with those flakes? Doesn't she ever wash her hair? I can't go a day without taking a shower and washing my hair. This girl looks like she's gone weeks, maybe months with no shower.

I really like my new shampoo and conditioner. They smell like pineapple and coconuts. Really delicious. I enjoy washing my hair. Why doesn't she wash hers? I feel like washing my hair right now!

Penny lets the line move up a bit before moving too. She puts more distance between her and the dandruff girl. Penny feels the breath from the geeky boy behind her. Every time he laughs, he breathes on Penny's neck. He is standing almost on top of her.

What is with this dude behind me? Laughing and snorting like a pig to himself. At least he's having some fun. Doesn't he know about personal space? He shouldn't be standing so close to me. I should let him stand right on top of Miss Smelly Hair. That would serve both of them right.

Penny finally makes it up to the lunch servers. The first server, a middle-aged woman with frizzy hair and wearing a tight fluorescent pink top asks,

"We have hamburgers or Caesar salad today. Which do you want?"

Penny quickly responds,

"I'll have the hamburger today, please."

The server grabs a pre-made hamburger from the heated tray behind the serving glass and puts it on a plate. She grabs a scoop full of mixed vegetables and dumps them next to the hamburger. Finally, she places an apple on the plate and hands it to Penny. Penny takes the plate and places it on her tray. Before she can even thank the woman for helping her, she is on to helping the geeky boy, who orders the Caesar salad while laughing to himself.

Penny grabs a container of milk, some utensils, salt, pepper, ketchup, and the chocolate chip cookies she was dreaming about and heads out of the kitchen area. She tells the "money lady" her account number and moves toward the seating area. She looks around to find her friends, who are sitting at their usual table today. Penny walks over and sits down near the middle of the table. Sitting at the table are Alyssa, Taylor, and Jenny. Also sitting at the table are some other girls who all three are "school friends" with.

"Hi guys! I thought I'd never make it here. There was so much traffic in the hallway, and the line took forever!"

Penny takes the top bun off her hamburger and sprinkles a little salt and pepper on top to try and give it some flavor. She squeezes some ketchup on top of the grey patty and drops the top bun back on. She picks the hamburger up and takes a big bite out of it. Ketchup shoots out the opposite end and lands on the table next to her tray.

Without giving it much thought, she grabs a napkin and wipes the ketchup up. As she gets the final wipe in, she notices that someone wrote on the lunch table. She shifts her tray a bit to the right so she can read what it says. Penny goes into shock as she understands what is written on the table – "Penny the pickle."

Penny slides her tray over the writing so no one can see it. She feels her face turn red and her heart starts to pound.

> *OMG, why is this here? Are they writing these things all over the place? Who is doing this? I have to do something to stop this! But what? What can I do to stop this? Whoever is doing this must know that. I can't believe this is happening to me! What am I supposed to do? Transfer schools? This is horrible.*

Penny's eyes start to water as she gets upset thinking about the graffiti and whoever is doing it. She chokes back a cry and pretends that she is having trouble with the hamburger in her mouth.

She lets out a low cough and wipes her eyes. She drops the hamburger on the plate and drinks her milk.

Jenny looks over at Taylor.

"Hey Taylor, are you coming to practice tonight?"

"I sure am. I want to meet our new team! Alyssa are you going?"

Alyssa, who is staring at a boy named Bobby Warstein, finally snaps out of her daze and answers.

"You bet. I'll be there. I packed up my gear last night. I'm all ready to go. Just need to change my clothes when I get home."

Jenny looks at Penny.

"Hey Penny, I know you must be coming tonight seeing how your parents are the coaches, right?"

Penny who is still thinking about the graffiti, and dealing with it in her head, is a bit startled when Jenny says her name.

"Uh… yeah… of course I'm going to be there. Why wouldn't I be there?"

"Well you don't sound too excited, Penny."

"Yeah…well, I was thinking about something else. I am excited. It's going to be a great year for us. I think we will really have a great team this year. We also don't have to deal with Coach Demon and all his crazy drills."

Taylor smiles and playfully punches Alyssa in the arm.

"At least we aren't on Dr. Leery's team! Right, Alyssa? Did you have fun playing for him for a few weeks last year? What a joke? I wouldn't want to have to go to his after-game meetings at his house to watch the videos he shoots of the games and review what every player did wrong. Or be forced to attend movie night. Although, I think you really liked those."

Alyssa responds,

"Get real. I was only on his team for a couple of weeks until my mom got me moved to Coach Devon's team. It wasn't that bad, but I have other things to do besides softball!"

The girls finish their lunches and start to get up to leave. Penny remains sitting. Alyssa taps Penny's shoulder.

"Hey, you ok? You look like something is wrong."

"No Alyssa, I'm OK. You go ahead. I'm going to be a few minutes. I want to finish this burger.

Everyone leaves and Penny takes the Sharpie she's been carrying with her since she first discovered the graffiti in the bathroom. She moves her tray to expose the writing, and quickly scribbles on top of it with the Sharpie.

I hope no one sees me doing this, especially the lunch ladies. If they see me, I'm going to get in big trouble. I will probably need to explain what is going on. That wouldn't be good at all.

Penny caps the marker and puts it back in her pocket. She shoves the hamburger into her mouth and almost eats the whole thing in one bite. She chokes down the hamburger. She almost forgets about the cookies she wanted to eat. She puts them in her pocket and returns her tray to the kitchen.

Chapter 5:

The entire Porter family arrives at Pine Hills town park for their first practice. They park the large black SUV close to the path that leads down to the field. Even the twins are excited.

Everyone hops out and Mr. Porter pops open the electronic tailgate. It rises with a pleasant-sounding chime to alert everyone it's opening. The family is immediately greeted with the smell of fresh cut grass. The sun is shining with only a few high wispy clouds in the light blue sky. The only sound they hear is a song playing from an ice cream truck somewhere nearby.

Mr. Porter starts unloading the softball equipment and places it on the parking lot pavement. The equipment includes three buckets of 12-inch bright yellow softballs, a couple of different size bats, a few gloves, a medical bag, a collapsible net, and a collapsible pitching screen.

The last item Mr. Porter takes out of the SUV is a large black cart. He loads all but the net and pitching screen in the cart. He instructs the twins to take those down to the field. Penny grabs the handle to the cart and pulls it quickly toward the dugout.

Mr. and Mrs. Porter follow behind the cart to make sure that nothing falls off. Many players and parents are already at the field. The players are in the dugout with their bags hung on the fence. Most are behind the bench, but a few are in front. Penny hears the girls talking, laughing, and giggling. The parents are sitting quietly chatting on the bleachers.

Penny wheels the cart on the field, near the dugout that her teammates are in. She parks it next to the pass-through in the fencing and grabs her bat bag from the cart. Just as she starts picking up her bag, she hears a few girls call her name. They even begin chanting it! Penny gets even more excited about this season.

She finds an open spot on the fence and hangs her bag behind the bench. Alyssa snakes her way through several players who are talking and high fives Penny.

"Hey Pens, how's it going? Did you hear about Karen?"

"No. Karen Wise?"

"Yep. That Karen. She was caught making out with a boy from the eighth grade! I think his name is Ben or Benny."

"Wow, Alyssa. Isn't she a bit young to be doing that? Who caught her?"

"I think it was her parents. Anyway – her parents know, and now she's grounded. She said she can't use her phone for a month and her parents won't let her play softball this year."

Just as Penny was about to respond, Coach Margo calls all the girls out onto the field,

"Let's go ladies! We need to get started. Bring your gloves and facemasks!"

A few more girls arrive and drop their equipment bags on the concrete floor of the dugout. They grab their gloves and masks and hurry out to the group gathering around the coaches.

Coach Matt starts off the pre-practice talk,

> "Hi Girls, Welcome to your new team. As our league is expanding, we were allowed to coach this year. I am Coach Matt, and this is Coach Margo. Some of you know us as Penny Porter's parents. We are here to teach you how to be better players and to get you ready to move up to play 14u next year. We will be practicing twice a week on Tuesdays and Fridays. No one should have any conflicts with practice as we are using the standard days that the league published last year."

Coach Margo takes over,

"You need to come to all practices. If you can't make it, you need to let us know as soon as possible. I know many of you learned to play softball last year and were taught by some of the other coaches in the league. However, we are going to now show you the 'right' way to do things. It may seem different and strange at first but trust us – it's the right way and the right way is the only way to do something."

"Always make sure to bring all of your equipment to every practice. Don't forget to bring water with you! It's going to be a hot spring and summer and you need to make sure you stay hydrated. If you usually drink a sports drink, you need to make sure you cut the drink in half with water. Never drink a sports drink out of the bottle without diluting it with 50% water. Take a clean, empty bottle and pour half into the new bottle. Then fill both with cold water. You can even put a few ice cubes in to keep it cold."

"Girls with long hair, make sure that you tie your hair back in a ponytail, so the hair doesn't distract you while you are practicing or playing."

"We will be getting new uniforms this year. Something completely different from past years. We have a new team name as well – this year we will be the Pine Hills Flames!"

Coach Margo bends down and takes something out of a bag at her feet.

"This is our new jersey! Our team colors will be red, white, and blue."

When the players see the bright, new red jersey top with a giant Flames logo written in script across the front, they high five each other and jump up and down with joy. The girls start getting loud with their excitement. Coach Margo gets even louder and tries to speak over the players,

"Everyone will get a new uniform at one of our practices. Please take care of them. You will only get one uniform. We can't get another one."

"One more thing....."

Just as Coach Margo was about to start a new topic - a loud, noisy, blue beat-up pickup truck with giant tires roars into the park and comes to a screeching halt right next to the Porter's SUV. Even though it sounds like the truck's muffler is broken, the team can hear loud music playing in the pickup truck from more than two-hundred feet away.

The car door opens, and the music gets even louder. A girl dressed all in black, steps down from the tall truck holding an old glove, and a bright new bat. Her wavy long dark hair blows in the wind and at times covers her face as the wind changes direction.

As the girl gets closer, Coach Margo yells out to her,

"Let's go! You're late. Hustle!"

The girl moves more quickly and joins the circle. Coach Margo continues,

> "As I was saying….. take care of your uniforms. Also, I want to make sure that everyone understands that this is a TEAM. I won't allow any cliques to form or for bullying of any type. You are all teammates. Everyone needs to get along. We are all different. That is no reason for any one of you to make fun of another teammate. Anyone who bullies another player will be thrown off the team."

> "OK, now that my speech is over, and everyone is here, everyone needs to introduce themselves. Tell everyone your name and how many years you have been playing softball."

Penny goes first and introduces herself. They go around the circle introducing themselves and get through all eleven players. The girl who came to practice late goes last. As she says her name, Sue Stone, she looks down at her feet. Her voice is so low that it's hard to hear. The other girls look her over and start evaluating her. She tells the team that she has been playing softball for at least five years.

Coach Matt has the girls put their gloves and masks on the third base foul line. He then directs them over to the first base side of the field and has them start working on dynamic stretches. Coach Margo appoints Jenny to lead the stretches. Once they are done, Coach Margo instructs the girls to run the field — starting at home plate, going down the first base line all the way to the outfield fence, over 200 feet away, then along the fence to left field, and turning to run down the third base line all the way back to home plate.

Once they are done, Coach Matt tells them to go get a drink and come back out to the field in 3 minutes. Coach Matt turns to Margo and asks,

> "What's the story with the new girl? What's her name? Sam? I couldn't hear what she was saying."

"Her name is Sue Stone. She just moved to our area a few weeks ago. She seems quiet. Maybe she's shy. She did all the warmups correctly, although she was at the back of the pack when they were running."

The team comes back out on the field and they grab their gloves and masks. Coach Matt opens one of the buckets holding softballs. He instructs the girls,

"Partner up with someone. We have an odd number of girls on the team so one girl will have to join another group and throw three-way. Each group needs to get one ball."

The players hustle over to partner up and grab a softball. All, except for Sue Stone. She walks over to the coaches slowly and asks,

"Where should I go Coach?"

Coach Margo responds,

"Is everything alright, Sue?"

"Yes, Coach. Everything is fine."

Sue responded with her head down and avoided eye contact with the coaches. In as cheery a voice as he could muster, Coach Matt says,

> "Why don't you pick out whichever group you want to join and then ask if you can throw with them. I'll watch you. If there's any problem, I will come over and help. I'm sure any group will be happy to throw with you!"

Coach Matt watches Sue Stone slowly walk over to the first group, which is Penny and Taylor, and then asks if she can throw with them. Sue goes over to Penny's side and they begin throwing – Penny to Taylor, Taylor to Sue, Sue to Taylor, and then Taylor to Penny to complete the first round. Coach Margo instructs the team,

> "Try to only use your wrist to throw the ball for the first part of the warmup. Isolate your wrist. You can put your elbow on top of your glove if you want. Stay about six to eight feet apart and only use your wrist."

After a few minutes, Margo continues,

> "Ok, players on the foul line stay where you are. Players on the field side, back up about ten feet. Throw the ball easy and warmup your elbow and shoulder."

Coach Matt comes over to Margo,

> "Well she throws pretty well. I guess she wasn't lying when she said she has played for over five years."

After a few minutes, Coach Margo has the team back up another ten feet. After a few more minutes she yells out to the team,

> "OK, back up about twenty feet and throw the ball as high as you can. Make sure you throw over the top. Try to get the ball in an arc to your partner."

Coach Margo notices one of the new girls, Andrea Wilson, not throwing over the top and goes to help her do the drill correctly. After the coaches are happy with how everyone is throwing, they call the team in. Coach Matt tells the girls to get some water and then come back out for infield drill.

Most of the team comes right back out. All except for Erica Muller and Julia Philips. They both stay in the dugout whispering to each other. Penny, who is joking around with Alyssa notices the two in the dugout.

"Hey Alyssa, what are those two doing?"

"I don't know, but they keep on looking over here. Maybe they're telling secrets. Maybe they're talking about KAREN WISE!"

"Well if they were, why wouldn't they do it with the rest of the team? Why are they whispering and looking at us?"

Finally, the two gossipers from the dugout come out and join the rest of the team. The coaches run through infield drills and close out the first practice with some batting practice. Coach Margo works with the players to correct their swings, hoping to make them better hitters.

Chapter 6:

The next day, Penny comes home from school as usual. It was a fairly routine, uneventful day. However, this time after saying hello and giving her mom a kiss on the cheek, she announces,

> "Mom, I'm going to the park to have a catch with Alyssa and Jenny. I'll be back around six."

> "OK, Penny. Don't get in any trouble. Dinner will be at 6:30."

Penny goes into the garage, grabs her bat bag, which is more of a backpack with her bat sticking out of a side pocket. She slings the bat bag over her shoulder and runs out the door. Penny remembers that she has to close the door and runs back to hit the button that makes the garage door opener, close the door.

She hops on her old red bicycle and quickly peddles off toward the park. The Pine Hills park is just around the corner from the Porter's house, but it still takes about ten minutes to get there by bike. Once she arrives at the park, Penny carefully hops the curb on her bike and rides on the grass all the way down to their practice field.

As she approaches the dugout, she slows down and gets off her bike. She drops the bike on the ground and runs around the fence to go in the dugout with her friends. Alyssa turns toward Penny and her face lights up,

"What's up, Pens?"

Before Penny can answer, Jenny jumps into the conversation,

"Any more artwork? Have you figured out who did it?"

"No, things have been quiet the past couple of days. I still don't have a clue who could have done it. Nothing strange happened in school."

Taylor high fives Penny,

"Well, that's good news. At least it seems to have stopped. Maybe whoever did it got in trouble or moved away."

The girls grab their gloves out of their bags and Penny supplies a ball. They have a four-way catch. After a few minutes they mostly stop throwing and just talk. Taylor has an idea,

"Why don't we go down to the pond and hang out."

The girls gather their stuff up and walk over to the pond. Penny walks her bike over. Once they arrive at the pond, Penny drops her bike again on the ground. The girls sit on the grass. Taylor has her legs crossed and stares off at the pond. Alyssa lays down in the grass and is throwing a small rock she found up in the air and then catching it. Penny plops herself on the grass and looks over at Jenny, who is trying to pull something out of the pond.

Jenny gives up trying to pull the oddly shaped stick out of the pond as she realizes that her sneakers are now all muddy. She moves away from her friends and begins wiping the sides of her sneakers on the grass in an attempt to clean them. After a few minutes, she shrugs her shoulders, gives up, and rejoins her friends. She takes her sneakers off and leaves them by her softball bag, hoping they will dry by the time they leave. She sits down on the grass and starts picking at some of the clover growing in between the blades of grass.

Taylor grabs a few sticks nearby and breaks off a piece and lobs it into the pond, trying to get it toward the center. Alyssa sees this and stands up. She looks at the rock she has been tossing in the air, has an idea, and skims it across the water, throwing it sidearm. It takes three hops on the water before falling into the pond with a small "bloop" sound.

The girls were all enjoying their time in the park, getting some sun and being a part of nature. The temperature was just right – not too hot and not too cool either. The pond has a pleasant smell – kind of a mossy, mushroomy type of smell. It smells like earth and food and what you might imagine the color green should smell like. Jenny looks over at her sneakers drying in the sun and breaks the silence,

> "So, did any of you notice that girl yesterday? The one in the loud pickup truck? Penny, wasn't that the same girl who tripped all over the place at the Sports Source the other day?"

> "Yeah, I think that WAS her."

Jenny faces toward Alyssa and Taylor and tells them what happened,

> "So, get this - this freak of a girl comes into Sports Source the other night. Penny and I were in there getting new softball equipment. The door opens and this weirdo falls through the front door making a total racket. Then she tries to stop herself from falling and looks like a zombie or something. She looked ridiculous. Come to think of it, she was wearing dark clothes then too, just like she wore to practice."

Alyssa replies,

"Yeah she creeps me out a bit. Dark hair, dark clothes. She didn't say two words the whole practice."

Thinking back on throwing with the mystery girl, Taylor says,

"Penny and I warmed up throwing with her. She has a pretty good arm. She did the high arc drill pretty well. She got the ball to me almost every time. But you know – other than asking if she could throw with us, I don't think I heard her speak at all during practice. Do you think there's something wrong with her?"

Alyssa, who is always making fun of new kids, joins in,

"Yeah, maybe she's a spaz witch – you know falling down and always wearing black."

Alyssa laughs to herself, and continues on,

"I wonder where she keeps her witch's hat and broom. Maybe her bat doubles as her broom and she rides it around at night over all of our houses, casting spells on all of us."

Alyssa grabs a stick and rides it around like a horse. She laughs out loud and continues with her imaginary scenario as she dances around,

"Go broom, go! Hey, if she hits a home run every at-bat, maybe it's the broom doing it? Maybe she uses witch's magic to play softball. We should change the name of our team from the Flames to the Witches – the Pine Hills Witches. We can get orange and black uniforms. When we win a game, we give the other team candy…. Kind of like Trick or Treating…. We can keep a jack-o-lantern in the dugout as our mascot… Maybe play haunted music in between at-bats… Say spells and make charms. Maybe we come out for warmups during games in sheets with holes cut out for the eyes. We could be a team of ghosts to start. You know? That would be kinda cool."

Alyssa stops riding the stick and uses it like a bat to hit imaginary balls pitched to her. Jenny takes over,

> "Do you think she lives in a castle? Does she sleep in a coffin like a vampire? Hey, wait maybe she's a vampire, not a witch?"

Taylor stops playing with her long, light brown, straight hair and sets Jenny straight,

> "Jenny don't be stupid. Of course, she's not a vampire, we've seen her in sunlight. So, she must be a witch. She could be a clumsy, stupid, socially awkward witch – but still a witch, right?"

Penny stays out of the conversation, not wanting to get involved in Alyssa's fantasies and making fun of other kids. It's something that Alyssa has done since she was in kindergarten. She has gotten better at it over time – or worse depending on how you look at it.

Taylor not wanting to be outdone by Alyssa,

"Did you guys notice her long, dark wavy hair? Is it black or brown?"

Jenny responds,

"I don't know – it looks black to me. You know, like witch's hair."

Taylor continues,

"It's all over the place and covers her face too. She looks like some kind of hairy monster. Maybe she's a wolf-woman? I once saw a movie with a guy who turns into a wolf - except his hair was brown. He was a kid that turned into a wolf. He even played basketball. See? He played basketball and she plays softball!"

Taylor turns to the side, and lets out the best wolf howl she could do,

"Ahhhh-ooooooooooooh."

Taylor howls while chasing Alyssa around. After a few minutes, she gets tired and falls down to the grass laughing. Everybody laughs including Penny, who finally says something while laughing,

> "Taylor you look ridiculous! What happened to her being a witch?"

Alyssa jumps in,

> "See? I knew you'd believe it. She must be a witch alright!"

More seriously, Jenny speaks up,

> "Hey Pens, any chance she's the one drawing the funky graffiti about you?"

Penny considers the question,

> "I don't think so, Jenny. I don't even know her. Why would she say anything about me?"

Then Penny wonders if Sue Stone could be responsible for the graffiti,

> *Wow.....I didn't even think of that. Maybe she is the one who has been writing all that stuff about me. I think I've seen her in the bathroom by my science class before. I think*

I've even seen her sit at the same table we use, although she has lunch the period before we have it.

Jenny responds,

"Well you do have quite the reputation, striking all those players out last year. Maybe she didn't know she was going to be on our team. Once she found out, she stopped with the graffiti."

"I guess it's possible, Jenny. Anything is possible."

Taylor gets up again and decides to tackle Alyssa to the ground. Just as she jumps on Alyssa, she says in a spooky, giggly voice,

"Who knows what lurks in the hearts of a Stone."

Chapter 7:

"Penny!"

Mrs. Porter calls out from the kitchen. Penny, not wanting to get yelled at for not responding, returns the yell,

"Coming!"

She runs down the steps two at a time and almost performs a superhero landing when she leaps off the last couple of steps onto the cool, tiled floor. Her socks slide a little as she stands up and tries to get traction on her way to the kitchen. She knocks into a picture hanging on the wall and stops to make sure it doesn't fall off.

> *Whoa! I keep hitting this dumb picture. I hope it doesn't fall again. Last time, Dad had a fit with me. Sure, it's a picture of Grandma and Grandpa when they were younger, so I get why he would be angry... Oh, OK – I stopped it from swinging and it's not going to fall. That's good.*

I wonder what Mom wants. Probably something to do with the twins and their school. It's always about the twins.

Penny trots into the kitchen and finds her mother sitting at the kitchen table looking through some old pictures.

"Penny, I found this old book of pictures from when I used to play Junior League softball. I thought you might like to see them. Oh look, that's me hitting a homerun."

Mrs. Porter points out a few pictures to Penny as she remembers what it was like to play softball all those years ago.

"Mom, do you think I'm weird? Am I a spaz or weirdo or something?"

Mrs. Porter stops looking at her pictures and faces Penny,

"Why would you ask me that? What's going on, Penny?"

"Nothing is going on. It's just that...... I don't know...... sometimes I wonder if I'm normal or a weirdo."

"Penny, of course you're normal. You're a smart, beautiful, funny, talented girl. Are you having a problem in school or with one of your friends?"

"Mom, what's the story with that new kid, Sue Stone? You know.... The one who came late to practice. The weird witch in the loud pickup truck.

"Are you having a problem with her, Penny?"

"No. When I was at the park, some of the girls were talking about her. They think she's a witch or something. She dresses all in black. She acts weird, and her father drives that rusty old, pickup truck while playing who knows what kind of loud music."

"You know Penny, I spoke with her father after practice. He called me to find out about our schedule. We got to talking and he told me a little about Sue and himself. He's actually a very nice man.

They recently moved to Pine Hills because her father moved his company to New York City. He manufactures guitar strings. It turns out he's somewhat of a famous guitar player and used to play gigantic concerts.

He drives a rusty pickup truck because he needs to park it at the train station as his company is in New York City. He doesn't want to leave a new car at the train station as it could get scratched and dented. He told me that he normally drives a very nice, new car, but he dropped Sue off straight from work and didn't have time to switch cars.

Sue is a very shy, quiet girl. Her father told me that she doesn't make friends easily. He hopes that she makes some friends on the softball team. The move hasn't been easy for her.

Sue's mother is still in Los Angeles selling their old house and finishing up packing the house. She won't be here with Sue for several months. Sue is very upset about not being with her mother.

Her father also told me that Sue is a very good softball player and was on a very good team in California. They practice year-round there, and Sue has already played in some showcase tournaments."

"Wow, Mom. I didn't know any of that. That makes some sense then. So, I guess she's not a witch after all?"

"No, she's not a witch. Just a shy girl who misses her mother. You should get to know her better before you decide if she's weird or not, Penny. I know you've heard the old saying, 'You can't judge a book by its cover.' Well, that certainly applies here too. If you get to know her, you might find that she's a really great kid."

"Mom?"

Mrs. Porter looks closely at Penny,

"What is it, Penny? Did you already have a fight with Sue Stone?"

Penny looks down at her socks and picks some lint off of one, trying to find the words to tell her mother about the graffiti.

"No, Mom, but there is something else going on...... I found.... I mean..... Someone..... I mean..... There was this girl....."

"Penny look at me. Calm down and just tell me what happened."

Penny tries looking at her mother but finds it difficult to admit that she must have an enemy out there.

"Well, I was in the bathroom and I found my name scribbled alongside of a picture of a pickle. It says Penny the Pickle."

Mrs. Porter almost lets out a weak laugh, not realizing the complexity of the situation.

"Penny, kids and sometimes adults can be mean. There's no reason to get all upset over this. It's probably a joke or someone who is jealous of you."

"I also found another one on the lunchroom table. Right where I sit! It was so …."

Mr. Porter enters from the side door. He takes his coat off, and quickly throws it on top of the clothes dryer,

"Hey everyone…."

"Not now, Matt. We're discussing something important."

"Well, not as important as what I have to tell you!"

"What is it Matt?"

"I was just speaking with the Junior League regional director, Marilyn DeSantis. She said that our local Junior League is now entered into the Junior League World Series. For our age group, we are eligible to compete for the New York State Championship!

She said the Summer Ball championship is going to be held in Buffalo this year with some special events around Niagara Falls.

That would mean a road trip for the entire team. We would all need to stay in a hotel and have dinners out together. It would be like a vacation we take with the whole team!"

Penny's mood turned from nervous and somber to one of extreme excitement,

"Wow, Dad! Do you think we have a shot?"

"Penny, you keep pitching the way you've been doing, and the sky is the limit!"

Mrs. Porter also becomes excited and puts her photo album down on the table and stands up.

She takes Penny's hands in hers and they both start jumping up and down, a sort of ritual they have together when they are both excited about something.

"Matt, when does this take place?"

"Well, it's after our regular season is over. It starts the beginning of June, with local games starting mid-June. The first round of games has its own championship — for our local district - district 11.

If our team wins the district, we go on to play the winners of the other districts on Long Island. That's called the Section championship. If we win that, we go to Buffalo to play the winners of the other sections in New York state."

"Wow, Dad, that's amazing! I can't wait to tell the others on the team. It's OK if I tell them, right?"

"Sure. Just remember, our team will have to work and practice very hard to be successful and have a shot at playing Summer Ball."

Penny skips out of the kitchen, down the hall, up the stairs, and into her bedroom. She launches herself onto her bed and ends up rolling over and facing the ceiling.

> *It's kind of late to call everyone. I want to call Alyssa, Taylor and Jenny! They can call the others on the team to let them know. I wonder who is going to call that Sue Stone girl? Not me.*

> *I wonder if we can get rid of that Stone girl if she isn't a good player. Can we transfer her to another team? Mom says she's supposed to be a good player, but I've heard that before. Most kids who are supposed to be good, downright stink!*

> *Hmmmm. I wonder if there's any chance she's the one who created the graffiti about me? She sure is weird enough. If she's a witch, it would be easy for her....*

Oh wait, Mom said I should get to know her first before deciding if she's weird or not. She also said that Sue Stone is 'not a witch, just a shy girl who misses her mother.' So, I guess I shouldn't pass judgement on her yet until I get to know her better.

Chapter 8:

Penny finishes the few small assignments she has for homework. It takes her no more than a half hour, while sitting at the kitchen table. She gets up, stretches, and decides what to do next.

"Mom, I'm going to the park for a little while."

"Ok, Penny, but don't be too long. We're having lasagna tonight and it will be ready in about an hour."

"Ok, I won't be long. I don't think anyone is there anyway."

Penny grabs her softball backpack and hops onto her bike and pedals her way to the park. It's a damp, dreary afternoon. It rained earlier in the day, and although the rain stopped, the clouds are still in place. The smell of earth, grass, and moss are in the air. She hops the curb as usual and coasts down the slight hill toward the softball field. The damp grass makes the journey a bit slick.

Just as I thought..... no one is here.

Penny stops heading toward the field and instead heads toward the pond. She pedals her way to the spot where she and her friends were goofing around the other day. She notices a lone figure down by the wooden dock that was built to let people go a few feet out into the pond.

Penny doesn't think much of it and drops her bike nearly in the same place she did the other day. She takes another look over at the person on the dock but can't make out if it's a boy or girl, let alone who it is.

I have no idea who that is. Well......whatever. I guess I'll have a catch by myself.

She opens her backpack and grabs her glove and ball. She leaves the backpack on top of her bike, so it doesn't get wet. She walks a few feet away and throws the ball up in the air and catches it in her glove. She tries throwing the ball higher and higher.

Mom told me to get under the ball.

She moves around in a very loose circle throwing and catching the ball.

I guess I'll throw one last one and then go back home. No one is going to come here today.

Penny grabs the ball and rockets it skyward one last time.

OK...... I got it.... Just gotta get under it like Mom said.

Penny gets under the ball, but she goes just a bit too far, so the ball is almost past her head. She tries to adjust but it's too late. The ball hits her near the bridge of her nose.

Oww! Oh no. What did I do?

Penny drops to the ground. She shakes her glove off and checks her nose with her fingers. Blood starts running freely down her chin and pooling on her pants. She doesn't know what to do and starts to panic.

> *What am I going to do? I don't have any tissues or napkins! I can't believe this happened. I should have put my facemask on! That was really stupid.*

Just as Penny starts to get frantic searching through her backpack for something.... anything to help stop the bleeding, a voice of help calls out,

> "Here. Use this. Don't worry. They're clean."

The figure hands Penny a wad of tissues. Penny, who is on the ground, looks up and sees a hazy dark figure. She grabs the tissues and presses them to her nose, hoping the bleeding stops. As she moves her head up and tries to throw her neck back as she has seen other kids do, she gets a better look at the person who gave her the tissues.

> *I can't believe it – it's Sue Stone!*

"Penny, put your head forward and pinch across your nose."

"Sue, are you sure? I've always seen kids put their heads back."

"Penny trust me. I took a first aid course. Putting your head back is wrong. It makes the blood go down your throat, which can make you hurl."

Penny decides to listen to Sue since she seems so sure that what she is saying is correct. She puts her head down and pinches her nose.

"It's OK, Penny. It should stop in a minute or two. If it doesn't, I can run to your house and get your mom and dad to come get you.

Don't talk. Just keep your head down and pressure on your nose. The pressure makes the bleeding stop."

After a few minutes, Penny lifts her head up and looks at Sue who is kneeling down on the ground next to Penny. Sue puts her hand on Penny's shoulder and asks,

"Has it stopped yet? Let's see."

Penny takes the wad of tissues away from her nose. The bleeding stopped!

"Oh wow. You were right, Sue. The bleeding stopped!"

"Let's look at your nose. Here, look directly at me Penny."

Sue gives Penny's nose a good look, and proclaims,

"Hey, I'm no doctor, but it doesn't look broken or anything. Probably just a bad nosebleed."

Penny smiles at Sue.

"Sue, where did you learn all this first aid stuff?"

"I took a first aid training program at my old school in California. They offered a class for extra credit, so I took it. It seemed like it would be useful."

"Well, it definitely was useful! You saved me … and my nose! So, I heard your dad is a musician. He plays guitar or something."

"Yeah, he used to be in a rock band that toured around the world. They were pretty big I guess."

Sue starts to become shy and stares at the ground. She begins to realize that she is still kneeling next to Penny and gets up to her feet. Once she stands up, she goes back to staring at her feet.

Penny notices that Sue is uncomfortable and asks,

"Sue, you seem kind of shy. Is that why you always look down?"

"Yeah, I guess so. I don't have many friends and kids usually make fun of me. I had some problems back at my old school with being bullied. Once we moved here, I decided that would never happen again, so I try to keep my head down and out of everyone's way."

"Well you don't need to be shy around me. We're teammates and friends now."

"Thanks, Penny. That's great."

Sue smiles for a moment, but then her smile quickly disappears and she looks sad again.

"Sue are you alright? What's wrong? Did I say something bad?"

"No..... it's just.... I thought of something bad. It's not you or your fault."

"Is there something I can help with?"

"Well..."

Sue looking like she is about to cry, faces Penny and asks,

"If I tell you something will you promise to keep it to yourself?"

"Yes, of course. What is it?"

"I was taking the bus home from school last week and I found my name written on the seat. It said, "Sue has a heart like Stone. I don't understand…. I don't know many people here. Already, I must have made a bad impression. I tried to keep my head down, but apparently at least someone took notice of me… and not in a good way."

Penny is relieved to hear that Sue isn't upset over something she said. She is also relieved that she isn't the only one to have her name written on things.

"Sue, I know just how you feel."

"How could you? I've been trying very hard to keep to myself and not be on anyone's radar."

"Sue, I found my name on the wall in the bathroom as well as on the lunch table. I took a Sharpie and crossed both of them out. So, you aren't the only one to have their name made fun of. They called me a pickle. A pickle? I don't even look like a pickle!

It isn't right for whoever is doing this to make fun of us. We need to figure out who is doing this... and fast."

"Do you have any ideas on who it could be?"

"No, not for sure...at least not yet. But I'm working on it. I have some ideas."

"Is there anything I can help you with?"

"No, not right now, but if there is something, I'll be sure to let you know. We need to catch the nasty person doing this."

Sue and Penny continue to talk for about another hour. They enjoy each other's company and get to know one another.

Chapter 9:

The next day at school, Penny has a relatively easy morning and makes it through to lunch with no problems. She and her friends finish their lunches quickly and head outside to enjoy a little recess in the sun.

Jenny has a small pink "High-Bounce" ball with her. Including Alyssa, Taylor, and Penny, they have a 4 way catch. Sometimes they bounce it between themselves, other times, they throw the ball as a pop fly. The pink ball is difficult to catch as a pop fly as it bounces off of hands easily. The throws are easy so they can talk as they enjoy their catch.

"Hey Penny, when is our first game? Isn't it like in two or three weeks?"

"No Taylor, it's next Saturday."

"You think we'll be ready?"

"I sure hope so. I'm not worried about us, it's some of the others."

Alyssa changes the subject,

> "Do you guys see inside the cafeteria? That witch girl is sitting there reading a book. The book is kind of dark. I bet it's a book of spells. Maybe she's going to turn us all into black cats!"

Jenny offers her opinion,

> "I don't think she can pull it off. She's such a spaz. Besides, doesn't she need her cauldron and broom to cast a spell?

> You know.... Bubble, bubble, boil, and trouble."

Taylor corrects Jenny,

> "It's double, not bubble and toil, not boil."

> "What?"

> "It's double, not bubble and toil, not boil."

> "What are you talking about?"

> "The bubble, bubble thing. It's from Macbeth. Didn't you learn anything in

English this year? It's double, double, toil and trouble."

"OK, whatever, Taylor. Either way, I think she's casting a spell on us! Maybe instead of a PBJ in her lunch box, she has eye of newt, cat whiskers, garlic, and bird feathers! Maybe she even has a mini-cauldron in there."

Always ready to cause trouble, Alyssa jumps in,

"Garlic? What do you think she's doing? Chasing vampires?" Do you really think we have vampires here at Pine Hills? Oh, that would be cool! Maybe Mr. VanCott is a vampire! He always dresses weird and his skin is unusually pale, like he's never seen the sun!

Penny trying to put an end to the nonsense,

"First of all, Mr. VanCott would not be able to teach if he were a vampire. We've seen him during the day.

Second, Sue Stone is not a witch."

Jenny, not wanting to end the fun banter, throws the ball to Taylor and over talks Penny,

> "There's no way you know for sure that Sue Stone isn't a witch, or a vampire. Maybe she's both. Maybe she was a witch first and then got attacked by a vampire, the poor thing.
>
> Every time I look at her, she puts her head down and stares at her shoes. What kind of weirdo does that? I think she's hiding something. Like a dark little secret."

Penny decides to end this nonsense,

> "Look guys, she's not a witch. In fact, I was at the park yesterday and was talking to her."

Alyssa catches the ball and holds on to it. She walks closer to Penny wanting to hear more about the conversation with Sue Stone.

Penny continues,

"Since you guys weren't at the park, I decided to have a catch with myself. You know – throw the ball in the air and then catch it. Well I did that a bunch of times. I was just about to stop, so I threw the ball extra high. I messed up and the ball hit me in the nose.

I fell down and my nose started bleeding badly. I thought I was going to pass out. I looked in my backpack for something to use as a tissue. I couldn't find anything. Meanwhile, I'm bleeding all over myself.

I saw a figure on the dock, and it turns out it was Sue Stone. She ran over and handed me some tissues. I didn't know it, but Sue is trained in first aid. She told me exactly what to do to stop my nose from bleeding."

Jenny asks,

"So how does that prove she isn't a witch and casting spells over us? I hope you didn't let her take anything with your blood on it!"

Penny continues,

> "Well we got to talking and she's a really nice girl. She's shy, that's all. She had some issues in her old school where she was bullied. She doesn't want that to happen in Pine Hills, so she's keeping her head down.
>
> Also, her mother is still in California. She's totally missing her. She's having problems adjusting to being away from her."

Jenny adds,

> "Well she could still be a witch. After all she wears all that dark clothing."
>
> "C'mon Jenny. Give her a break. She's shy and lonely. You'd be a real peach if you didn't see your mom for several months – you know I'm right."
>
> "Well maybe a vacation from my mom is just what I need?"

"Jenny, you are so full of it. You and your mom are very close. You'd be lost without her."

"I guess you're right."

"I am right. Sue is now our teammate. We need to look out for her."

"I was wondering if she was the one responsible for carving your name in the bathroom."

"Oh, it's definitely not her. That's for sure. We can drop her from the list of suspects. I don't think I told you guys, but I found another work of art calling me a pickle."

Taylor moves closer to Penny,

"Where was this one? And no, you didn't tell us."

"It was on the cafeteria table. The one we sit at every day."

Maybe I shouldn't have said anything. Now I have to answer a million questions about it.

"What did it say?"

"Same thing. It looked the same as the other one. I crossed it out with my Sharpie. I really have to figure out who is doing this."

Not wanting to keep discussing her graffiti problem at recess, Penny changes the subject,

"Hey guys, with our first game on Saturday, we need to practice some new cheers. I found this one online. I thought we could use it. It goes like this:

My name is Penny and you know what I've got?

I've got a team that's hotter than hot.

Then everyone else says – 'How hot is hot?'

Doubles, triples, homeruns too!

Then everyone says – 'Uh huh uh huh.'

Now let's see what Alyssa can do!

We go around the whole bench so that all the players get to sing it. What do you think?"

Alyssa, not understanding why her name was called, has a confused look on her face. Jenny and Taylor understand how the cheer works. Jenny answers,

"Oh, that sounds pretty good. I heard another team do that once before, but I couldn't understand what they were saying!"

"I found a bunch of others. I was thinking about creating some sheets with the cheers on them. I can hand them out, so everyone knows the lyrics until we memorize them. I don't think it will take long."

"That one seems nice enough. Remember last year when we got yelled at by the umpire with the 'Hey pitcher, pitcher, tie your shoes' cheer? He said it was too aggressive toward the other pitcher. We should try to stay away from those. I don't want to get in any trouble for cheering."

"Yeah, let's keep it classy."

"If we beat them with our play, we don't need to beat them with our cheers too."

Chapter 10:

The girls are together in a circle. Coach Margo has their attention,

> "Ok girls today is our last practice before our season opener tomorrow. Is everyone ready for our first game?"

The team cheers with enthusiasm. Most of the girls either high five each other or pump their fist in the air. Coach Margo continues,

> "We've only had a few weeks of practice, but you girls have worked hard and are starting to really look good. Not great, mind you….. just good. Let's work hard today so you can look 'great' tomorrow.
>
> Take your fielding positions. Don't forget your masks – we don't want to damage any of those pretty faces! We switch on three – don't forget and be a field hog!"

Coach Margo refers to the process of players rotating in and out of their position every three plays during practice if they share their position with other players.

Penny heads out to the pitcher's circle. Taylor stays at home plate as the team's starting catcher. Jenny goes to center field. Alyssa goes to shortstop. Erica Muller, the backup pitcher goes to first base. Julia Philips, the number three pitcher goes to third base. Andrea Wilson goes to second base. Kayla Kim goes to right field. Mary Mooney goes to left field. Deb Branford, the backup catcher stands off to the side near first base, as an alternate first baseman. Sue Stone stands off to the side near left field as an alternate outfielder.

Coach Margo calls out what the imaginary field situation is,

"There's no out, and no one on."

Most of the team immediately calls out,

"Play to first."

Coach Margo hits the ball to Alyssa at shortstop, who runs toward the ball, fields it cleanly on the first hop, steps toward first, and fires the ball over to Erica on first almost on a straight line. Erica stretches her glove on her left hand to where the ball is thrown and makes a clean catch while the toes on her right foot are touching the first base bag. She immediately comes off the base and throws the ball to Taylor near home plate. Coach Matt yells out,

> "Great job. That looked very clean. Alyssa the transition from fielding to throwing could have been faster. Please start making the transition to throwing as soon as you have possession of the ball, but definitely before your step toward first is complete."

Alyssa gives a thumbs up to Coach Matt and resets herself in her ready position. Coach Margo calls out the next play,

> "Runner on first, one out."

Like clockwork, the team yells out almost in unison,

"Play to two, get the lead runner."

Coach Margo hits the ball down the third base line. It's a choppy ground ball that is hit just inside the third base foul line. Julia charges the ball and catches it almost on the ground. Her glove is full of dirt. She pivots and takes a step toward second base. The movement is slightly awkward as she needs to throw over her left shoulder if she doesn't pivot.

As Julia begins pulling her glove up, a stream of dirt that she scooped up while fielding the ball begins to fall out and scatter in the wind. She fires the ball over to Andrea Wilson playing second base. Andrea did not start to move over to cover the second base bag quickly enough when the ball was hit and is late getting near the base. She catches the ball in her glove but drops it as she tries to recover her balance.

Coach Matt yells across the field,

> "OK, Julia, nice job not letting that ball get past you. Nice pivot as well. Try not to get so much of the field in your glove next time!

Andrea, you need to break for second base immediately if the ball is hit to the left side of the field."

Andrea nods her head in acknowledgement and moves back to her position between first base and second base. Coach Matt says in a low tone to Coach Margo,

"Hit two again."

This indicates that he wants Coach Margo to make the play to second again. She in turn yells out,

"Same situation. Runner on first, one out."

Once again, the team responds,

"Play to two, get the lead runner."

This time, Coach Margo hit a line drive directly to Andrea. Instead of making a play, Andrea moves to the side to avoid the ball. Coach Matt looks at Coach Margo and they just stand for a long pause looking at each other. Finally, Coach Margo drops the bat and walks over to Andrea.

"Hey Andrea – are you OK?"

"Yes, Coach. I'm OK."

"You know you were supposed to catch the ball, right?"

Andrea nervously chuckles,

"That thing was like a rocket. No way I'm going to catch that."

"Andrea, what positions do you normally play?"

"Well Coach, I've only ever played outfield. Usually left field."

"Ok."

Coach Margo walks back to home plate. She is met by Coach Matt. They turn their backs to the field and face the back stop. Slowly they both walk toward the fencing that creates the back stop. Coach Matt asks,

"So, what did she say?"

"She said that she knew she was supposed to catch the ball but there was no way she was going to catch it because it was a 'rocket.' I didn't even hit it that hard. She also said that she normally plays outfield — usually left field."

"How does she do on outfield drills? Can she drop step?"

"Yeah, I think she did pretty well in outfield drills. She tracks pretty well."

"OK, so we should let her stick with that then. Why did we have her at second?"

"We don't have anyone else."

"Not good…. what about….. no, that won't work……. what about…. the Stone girl?"

"I guess so. Let's try her."

Coach Margo cups her hands to her mouth to form a type of megaphone,

"Andrea to left. Sue to second."

Andrea begins running to where Sue Stone was standing. However, Sue hesitates and then slow jogs toward second. Coach Margo speaks to her players on the field,

"OK. Same situation. Runner on first, one out."

Once again, the team responds,

"Play to two, get the lead runner."

Coach Margo hits the ball to third again. Julia stumbles a little with her footwork but recovers and fields the ball cleanly on the second hop. She pivots as before and makes the throw to Sue playing second.

Sue, who immediately sprinted to second base when she saw the ball was hit to the left side was positioned correctly and made a good play. Coach Matt praises,

"Great job, Sue."

Coach Margo smiles and calls the next play,

"OK. Same situation. Runner on first, one out."

As expected, the team immediately responds,

"Play to two, get the lead runner."

Coach Margo hits a fly ball directly at Sue. She stays her ground, makes the catch, transfers the ball to her throwing hand and fires it over to Erica at first base, simulating a double play. Coach Matt and Coach Margo both look at each other again and smile. Coach Matt speaks quietly, but with enthusiasm to Coach Margo,

"I think we found our new second baseman."

He then yells out,

"Great job, Sue. Way to go. Double play!"

The rest of the practice goes well. They practice hitting. Pitchers and catchers go first, then pitchers warmup and throw all of their pitches. Penny pitches great. Afterwards, Taylor and Deb work on their throwdowns.

As practice nears the end, Coach Margo calls all the players together in an end of practice circle. She brings a large box with her.

"Great job today everyone. I think we are going to have a great game tomorrow. We face the Teawork Titans. They are travelling a long way to get to the field. We should be fresh and have the advantage..... but only if you focus on having fun and on making plays. Our hitting is usually excellent, so that should take care of itself. We know their pitcher. We've faced her before. She throws well, but nothing we can't hit.

Warmups are at 8:30am. That means you need to be there by 8:15am. Don't be late. Anyone who comes late will bat last. Bring plenty of cold water! It's going to be warm tomorrow.

Hands in......Alyssa take us out!"

Alyssa shouts loudly,

"All hands in.... Pine Hills Flames on three. Ready. One. Two. Three!"

All of the players yell,

"Flames!"

Coach Margo looks down at the box,

"Oh, I almost forgot……. Here are your new uniforms! Everyone needs to make sure they get the right size pants and jersey they ordered. If you forgot the size you ordered, Coach Matt has the list. Also be sure to get a pair of socks."

The players all get their uniforms and pack up their equipment. Coach Matt and the twins loads the cart and begin the trek to the car. Julia and her mother hang around the bleachers and wait for Coach Margo and Penny to walk by. Julia's mother, Mrs. Philips puts her hand out and says to Coach Margo and Penny,

"Coach, do you have a minute?"

"Sure, Donna. What's up?"

"Well, Julia came home from school today and was upset by a conversation she had. Julia – why don't you tell the story?"

Julia, who is clearly nervous speaks in a low, shaky voice,

"In the cafeteria today, I sat next to Erica. She was in a bad mood and was saying how she wasn't sure if she wants to go to practice today."

"OK, maybe she wasn't feeling well."

Coach Margo reasons, trying to come up with a valid excuse why Erica would not want to attend practice. Julia, speaks louder, wanting the coach to understand what she is saying,

"No Coach, that isn't it. That isn't it at all. She said...."

Julia turns toward Penny and then looks away again,

"She said that she hates Penny. She isn't sure if she should even play for on our team. She thinks that she won't get any playing time as the backup pitcher."

Coach Margo's eyes got very large with surprise. Penny, in shock, begins to understand, and puts the pieces together in her head. Julia continues,

"While we were sitting at the lunch table today, she scratched your name into the table with a red pen. I saw your name, but I couldn't read what else she wrote."

Ohhhh. So that's who wrote the graffiti about me! Now I know. Why does she hate me though? We used to be such good friends.

Coach Margo addresses Julia,

"Thank you for stepping forward Julia, you did the right thing by coming to us with this."

Chapter 11:

Coach Matt looks at his watch again. It's now 8:20am and the players are all supposed to be at the field by 8:15am. Everyone but Sue Stone came on time. Coach Matt speaks to the team,

> "OK ladies, let's take the first base side dugout."

The girls form a line and walk into the first base dugout. They hang their backpacks behind the bench. The catchers drop their gigantic equipment bags in the corner of the dugout. Coach Matt puts two buckets out on the field along with a practice net in a bag. Coach Matt thinks to himself,

> *It's going to be a hot one today! It must be 85 degrees already. Should be in the mid-90's by lunch time.*

> *Lunch! Boy those hot dogs sure smell delicious! I'm going to get one before we leave the park today.*

Coach Matt checks his watch again, it's now 8:30am. Coach Matt wonders,

> *Where is that girl? I guess we have to go with Andrea on second base. We didn't have time to try anyone else out.*

Coach Matt walks over to Coach Margo who is now on the field sizing up the other team. He quietly speaks to her,

> "Sue Stone still isn't here. What do you think? Is she going to come?"

> "Her dad said he was excited to see her play again. He knows the game is today and he emailed back that she is able to make it. She should be here. Maybe they got stuck in traffic?"

> "OK, but what are we going to do if she doesn't show? Are we putting Andrea back at second? Our only other choice is Deb Branford, but we've never had her play second before."

> "Well maybe we should ask."

Just as Coach Matt starts walking over to speak with Deb Branford, a loud rumble is heard, and a rusty blue pickup truck comes racing into the parking lot. The tires on the truck squeal making the turn into the lot. Hot fumes and dust emanate from under the pickup truck as it comes to an abrupt halt near the field.

Sue Stone jumps out in her Flames uniform and with her equipment bag. She runs through the parking lot, through the access path to the field and into the dugout. She looks at Coach Matt,

"Sorry I'm late Coach."

Coach Matt looks at his watch - 8:36, nods at Sue and yells to the team,

"OK everyone let's go. Bring your glove, bat, and facemask out with you. Line them up along the fence. To start, run to the right field fence and back, two by two. Stay together like a team!"

The team takes off in pairs, except for Sue Stone who is last and runs by herself. They complete their running warmup. Coach Margo waits for them as they return,

> "OK ladies do your stretches. Jenny take them out and lead the stretches."

The team runs out onto the right field grass and they do their dynamic stretch routine. They are finished in less than 10 minutes and return to the area they left their equipment. Coach Margo calls out the next warmup,

> "Grab a ball and partner-up. Warm up throwing. Don't be long, we need to warm up hitting and get our pitchers to warm up too."

The team heads out to the outfield again and they warm up their arms by throwing to each other. Coach Matt sits down on one of the buckets and creates the batting order. He consults with Coach Margo,

> "Here's what I'm thinking. Kayla Kim as lead off. She is our most reliable player to get on. Taylor is next. She can bunt. Erica in

third. She's been very good hitting lately. Alyssa as our cleanup hitter. Penny as our backup cleanup in fifth. Jenny in sixth. Julia in seventh. Mary Mooney in eighth. Assuming we're having Sue play second now that she's here, we put her at the bottom of the batting order in ninth. Deb and Andrea are the substitutes. We can get them in the game later. How does that sound?"

"Sounds about right. Let's go with that."

Coach Matt fills out his paperwork, including a copy of the batting order for the other team. By the time he completes his paperwork, the team comes in and is ready for hitting warmups. Coach Matt throws soft toss from the side, where the players hit into the net. Coach Margo throws front toss with weighted sand balls. All of the pitchers and catchers go first so they can go warm up pitching.

Once warmups are done, Coach Margo gathers the team together,

"OK ladies. Here we go. Here's what I expect in this game. Number one, I want you to have fun! Next, I want you to play like a team, not just a group of players. Anticipate what your teammates are going to do. Keep the communications high. Call out each play just like we do in practice. Catchers – you control the infield. You have the best view. Make sure you guide the infield where to make the play as the play evolves. Jenny, you're our center fielder. You control the outfield. Call the outfield plays. Waive off infielders trying to make popup catches in the outfield, if the outfield can make the play. Stay hydrated – it's warm out today. Finally, I want to hear cheering throughout the game. Keep your energy level high.

I also want to talk about one disturbing topic. We are a team. We play as a team. You need to back up your teammates. You won't like every player you will play with, but you do need to support every one of them. They are your teammates. Talking about teammates behind their back or carving their name in the bathroom wall isn't being a good teammate.

Be sure to back each other up. Let's go get 'em!"

The team goes into the dugout and gets ready for the game. Coach Matt goes out to the coach's conference at home plate and wins the coin toss. He selects to be the home team. This allows the Flames to bat last in case they are down in the score in the last inning.

He comes back to the dugout and informs the team that they are home team. He instructs them to take the field. The starting players start running out to their positions. Deb Branford and Andrea Wilson stay in the dugout. Erica is also still in the dugout. She looks troubled and walks over to Coach Margo,

"Coach, I'm not feeling well. I have a stomachache. I don't think I can play."

"Oh, I'm sorry to hear that Erica. Do you want to sit and see if it gets better, or do you want to leave?"

"I think I better leave."

"OK, I hope you feel better."

Erica packs up. Coach Margo assigns Deb Branford to first base. She grabs a softball and runs out to her position. The team warms up by throwing the ball around in a pre-set pattern: first base to second, short, and third. The pitcher warms up pitching with her catcher, and the outfield throws amongst themselves.

The game starts as a very competitive game. Both teams are evenly matched and the score going into the top of the fifth inning is zero-zero. Time is running out. The umpire announces that this will be the last inning.

Penny, who is getting a little tired after pitching four innings, takes a deep breath in the pitcher's circle ready to throw the first pitch of the fifth inning. Coach Matt gives Taylor the sign for the pitch he wants thrown. Taylor shows the sign to Penny. It's a fastball on the outside corner.

Penny brushes the sweat from her forehead, takes a deep breath and starts her motion. She throws the pitch. The Titans' number four batter smacks the ball up the middle back at Penny. It almost hits her square in the face. The ball comes back at her so fast and in a straight line so that Penny cannot judge where the ball is. She drops down to protect herself. As a result, the number four batter gets on first base. This is one of the few players to get on base in this game.

Penny brushes herself off and gets ready for the number five batter. This girl is tall and husky. She looks very strong. Penny receives the sign from Taylor and throws a perfect strike low and inside – strike one.

Penny composes herself by walking to the back of the circle. She looks over to Jenny and smiles. Jenny waves back at her and gives her the thumbs up,

"Here we go Pens, you've got this."

Penny gets in position on the pitching rubber and receives the sign. She throws a drop ball, hoping this one drops enough to fool the batter. The batter swings where the ball originally was, but it drops toward the ground too close to home plate for her to react to it – strike two.

Penny follows her ritual again of going to the back of the circle. This time she looks over to Kayla Kim in right field. Kayla waves back,

"C'mon Penny. You can do this!"

Penny returns to the pitching rubber and takes the sign from Taylor. It's a rise ball.

Oh boy. I hope my rise ball works today. It was a little shaky in practice! I wish Dad called for a curve ball instead. I would rather try to throw that!

Penny goes into her motion and releases the rise ball a little late. She throws a wild pitch over Taylor's head and into the backstop – ball one. The runner on first base, easily steals second base on the wild pitch.

Penny goes to the back of the circle, bends down, and picks up some dirt to dry her now sweaty hands. She returns to the pitching rubber and takes the sign from Taylor. Penny goes into her motion and throws a bullet of a pitch, high and outside. The batter was expecting a low pitch and could not adjust to it and misses it by a mile – strike three.

The Flames' fans go crazy and start screaming for Penny and the rest of the Flames!

Penny, back on the rubber, receives the next sign and takes a deep breath – a changeup on the first pitch! She starts her motion, with her arm going as fast as a fastball. She releases the ball and it seems to float. The number six batter doesn't have a chance – she swings what seems like a full second before the ball reaches the plate – strike one.

Penny goes to the back of the circle and looks over to Jenny in center field. Jenny gives her a thumbs up and pounds her right fist into the pocket of her glove. Penny returns to the pitching rubber and receives the next sign from Taylor – low and outside fastball. Penny goes into her motion and releases the ball. It's a beauty of a pitch. Perfectly placed and very fast. The number six batter not wanting to be fooled with a changeup again, hesitates just a fraction of a second, but long enough to see it's not a changeup. She makes contact with the pitch and rockets it back toward Sue Stone.

The runner on second base takes off for third base and passes Alyssa who is running to cover the second base bag.

Sue, who is ready for the ball, barely has to move, and makes the catch. The runner heading toward third puts on the brakes and tries to return to second base. Sue immediately flips the ball to Alyssa who is covering the second base bag. She steps on the base before the runner returns – double play!

The Flames' fans go wild. They cheer the team on and jump up and down on the bleachers making a racket. Sue smiles, knowing that her play just ended the Titans' chances of winning the game. Worst case - the game will end in a tie.

It's the last at bat for the Flames. The score is zero-zero, bottom half of the fifth and last inning of the game. The bottom of the batting order will have to get the job done! Up at bat for the Flames is Julia Philips, backup pitcher and third baseman. Julia holds her hand up to get in the batter's box.

As she holds her hand up, she looks over at Coach Margo, who gives her the hit away sign. Julia takes a check swing and enters the box. The Titans' pitcher throws a curveball that hits the outside corner – strike one.

Julia, who is now ready for the next pitch tries to figure out what the pitcher is going to throw. She guesses an inside pitch and backs away from the plate just slightly. Coach Margo gives her the hit away sign again. The pitcher throws an outside pitch and Julia, being a bit too far from the plate misses it – strike two.

Julia gets back in the batter's box and Coach Margo repeats the hit away sign again. The Titans' pitcher throws a changeup without giving away the pitch. Julia sees the pitch released and assumes a fastball. She swings way ahead of the pitch – strike three. One out.

Next up is Andrea Wilson, left field, who was substituted for Mary Mooney in the fourth inning. Andrea gets her sign from Coach Margo – bunt. Andrea stands up in the box as close to the pitcher as she can without going past the lines in the batter's box. The pitch is thrown, and Andrea drops down a bunt toward the third base foul line. She drops the bat and takes off toward first base. The ball slowly rolls into foul territory – strike one.

The Flames players on the bench get loud and start cheering Andrea on. They hope the strength of their cheers will bring Andrea strength to get on base.

Andrea jogs back to home plate and picks up her bat. She gets a signal from Coach Margo to bunt again. Andrea takes the same position in the batter's box. The pitch comes in and Andrea lays down a perfect bunt down the first base line.

However, the Titans' first baseman played up close to home plate after the previous bunt attempt. She grabs the bunted ball with her throwing hand and fires the ball over to first base. The throw beats Andrea to the bag – Two out.

The Flames know that their chances of winning the game rely on Sue Stone. They now have two out. If Sue can get on base, they can get to the top of the batting order and hopefully get something going.

Sue steps up to the batter's box. She holds her hand up and looks over to Coach Margo who gives her the sign to hit away. The pitch is thrown, and the ball is a pitcher's pitch – just at the knees or slightly below and over the plate – strike one.

Sue steps out of the box and takes a deep breath. The pressure is increasing, and Sue knows this is all coming down to her,

I can't believe that I have to be put in this position. My first game in Pine Hills and I get to have the honors of the last out. How does this happen! I'm going to look really

stupid if I strike out. The team is going to hate me if I miss this ball.

Sue looks over to Coach Margo for her sign – swing away again. She steps in the box with her hand up and positions her feet. This time she takes her time getting situated in the box. She looks up at the end of her bat and focuses on the numbers printed around the barrel. She spins the bat three times for good luck. She puts her hand down, indicating to the umpire that she's ready. The pitch is thrown and it's a changeup. Sue recognizes it as a changeup and holds off swinging – strike two.

How do I get myself into these jams? I only have one more chance to connect with this ball. I definitely need to swing at this next pitch.

Coach Margo calls time out and motions for Sue to come over for a conference,

"How are you feeling, Sue?"

"Good, Coach."

"OK, well you have two on you now. You need to swing at this next pitch if it's even close."

"I know, Coach. I was just thinking that."

"We really need you here, Sue. Look it's just a game, so relax, get a good read on the ball and if it's close drive it out. I believe in you."

"Thanks, Coach."

Coach Margo taps Sue on top of her batting helmet. Sue turns around and jogs back to the batter's box. She holds her hand up and gets back in the box. She looks up at the end of her bat again and spins it three times. She adjusts her feet and puts her hand down.

I can do this. I can do this.

Sue takes a deep breath and tries to relax like Coach Margo told her to do. The pitch is thrown and it's a high fastball — Sue's favorite pitch! Sue times the ball and swings. She makes contact on the sweet spot of the bat and drives the ball to deep right field, almost to the fence and close to the foul line.

She drops the bat and takes off for first base. She looks at Coach Matt at first base who is giving her signals to "keep going." Coach Matt is screaming,

"Hustle! Pickup Coach on third!"

Sue turns her head and sees that they are still chasing toward the batted ball and keeps running to second base. As she approaches second base, she looks over at Coach Margo who is giving her the "keep going" signal.

Sue steals a look toward right field and sees that the ball is being thrown to a cutoff. The Titans' second baseman positioned herself in shallow right field between first and second base. Sue focuses on getting to third base and looks at Coach Margo again, who is still giving her the "keep going" signal. Coach Margo screams,

"All the way, Sue! Slide into home!"

Sue gets a bit more than three-quarters of the way to home and sees the ball being thrown in.

The catcher who is standing to the left field side of home plate, is ready to make the catch and tag. Sue sees where the catcher is standing and adjusts herself to the left of the third base foul line. She begins her slide and sees the catcher catch the ball. The catcher starts moving toward Sue but doesn't wait long enough to get possession of the ball before trying to make the tag out. The ball pops out of the catcher's glove!

Sue is safe at home! The Flames win!

The team runs out of the dugout and the players greet Sue at home plate. They all jump up and down and scream. Coach Margo reminds the team to calm down, line up, and celebrate later. They line up along the first base foul line and practice the tradition of the after-game handshake, which is more of a hand wipe than a shake.

The coaches at the end of both lines greet each other. The Titans' coach congratulates Coach Margo,

> "That was an exciting, great game. That was a smart move putting a big bat at the end of

the lineup! I'm going to have to try that. We'll see you soon."

After the game is over, both teams line up on their respective foul lines again. A league official comes out and makes a short, but well-deserved presentation,

> "I want to congratulate both teams on a great game. That was really fun to watch. It was a nail biter until the very end.

> Both teams were very competitive and well-behaved. I saw some great sportsmanship on both sides today. I wish I could say that is always the case, but it isn't. You should all be proud of yourselves for that.

> This was a great way to open the season for Junior League Softball. We couldn't have asked for a better game, or two better teams.

> I want to award the Most Valuable Player award – the MVP to the player who made a spectacular double play in the top of the

fifth inning. That single play may have changed the outcome of the game. That wasn't the only thing this player did tonight. She also scored the only run in the game, and by way of homerun, no less.

This award was voted on by the Titans players and coaches. The MVP award goes to Sue Stone of the Pine Hills Flames!"

Sue blushes as she walks over to receive her award. The league official places the award, which is strung on a blue ribbon, around Sue's neck. She shakes the man's hand and is told to turn around so another league official can take a picture. Sue is left with one thought,

Wow! I did it!

Chapter 12:

The team goes out to Buddies for dinner and ice cream. Sue is still smiling. She can't stop smiling. She is so happy. Everyone wants to sit next to Sue. The team's level of excitement is still high. The moment is magical.

Penny, who is sitting at the end of the players' table, shouts over the loud restaurant to Sue,

> "Hey Sue, how ya feeling now?"

> "Great, Penny, Just great! I'm so glad my parents decided to move to Pine Hills!"

> "You know Sue, you look good in colors other than black – light colors make you look and feel happier."

> "Maybe I need to rethink my wardrobe. I like these colors. Want to help me go shopping?"

> "Sure. I have a great sense of fashion, but you probably already knew that!"

Sue who hasn't stopped smiling, laughs at Penny's comment.

The coaches and parents are sitting together at another big set of tables. Jenny's father, Al Carson stands up to make a toast with a Diet Coke in his hand,

> "Congratulations to our two amazing coaches – Margo and Matt. You guys did a great job with this team. We couldn't have ever dreamed of having a team like this last year.
>
> Many of us have been watching your practices and the way you handle the girls. We like that you give all of the players opportunity to practice positions other than what they normally play. You allow outfielders to play infield and vice versa.
>
> Your game strategy was excellent today as well. That was the tightest game I've ever seen. Penny pitched amazing today. What was it a one hitter?"

"Yes, she threw a one-hitter, shutout, with seven strikeouts."

"Outstanding!"

"On behalf of all of the families, I want to say thank you for coaching our girls."

The other parents raised their soft drinks, milk shakes, ice cream sodas, and root beer floats in agreement with the toast.

Coach Margo, realizing that she has not seen Penny in a while, looks over at the players' table. She sees that Penny is having fun and all the players are laughing and having fun but are not too loud.

As she turns her head back toward the adult table, she sees something odd. She turns back and has a better look. She sees Erica Muller and her family at a table having dinner.

That's odd. She said she wasn't feeling well a few hours ago. I guess her conscience got the best of her. The Mullers obviously know we are here, as the toast Al Carson gave wasn't exactly quiet, and the players are certainly raising the noise level in here.

Alyssa stands up and with her rather loud, playful voice and shouts out,

"Two...four...six...eight...

Who do we appreciate?"

The entire team, with the exception of Sue, shouts out,

"Sue...Sue...Yay, Sue!"

After a while, the players, parents, and coaches calm down and focus on eating their food. The Mullers finish their meal. Mr. and Mrs. Muller go to pay the bill. Erica makes her way over to the player table and waves over to Penny to come talk to her.

Penny gets up and meets Erica a few feet away from the table – just far enough so no one can hear what they are talking about. Penny, feeling a bit defensive, stands with her arms folded across her chest. Penny starts the conversation,

"You missed a great game. We won 1-0, in the bottom of the last inning."

"Yes, I kind of got the feeling that you guys won based on everyone being happy and smiling.

Look Penny, I'm sorry."

"Sorry for what?"

"Well, first, I'm sorry I left the game today. I shouldn't have done that. It was wrong. I actually did have a stomachache, but not because I wasn't feeling well. It was because I was nervous.

Which brings me to the second thing I'm sorry for. I wrote your name on the bathroom wall and on two cafeteria tables."

"Why would you do that, Erica? Do you know the panic you gave me?"

"I know. I'm sorry. It's just that I was really angry with you."

"You are angry with me?"

"Well, not anymore. But I was. I was until I talked to my mother and told her what I did and why I did it."

"So, why did you do it?"

"Well, ever since you started pitching, I became the number two pitcher. You seem to always start, and I seem to always sit and watch you. I also want to pitch.

When I spoke to my mother, she made me realize that sports are competitive. It's not only the teams competing with each other, but the players are also competing. This isn't a bad thing, it's a good thing as it helps the players push themselves to become better players.

So, you being the starting pitcher will actually push me to become a better pitcher, which in turn causes you to push yourself to become a better pitcher too."

"You know, I never really thought about it like that. That actually makes sense. Let me ask you something — Did your parents make you come over and apologize to me?"

"No. I realized that what I did was wrong. I feel really badly about it. I don't want to be enemies with you. We used to be such good friends. I hope we can be that way again."

"Sure, I'd like that."

"Congratulations on your win today — Penny Porter, the pitcher from Pine Hills!"